A Great Big Night

WORDS BY KATE INGLIS ART BY JOSÉE BISAILLON

NIMBUS
PUBLISHING LTD.
NIMBUS.CA

Nimbus Publishing Limited
3660 Strawberry Hill St, Halifax, NS, B3K 5A9
(902) 455-4286 nimbus.ca

Printed and bound in Canada
NB1395
Design: Heather Bryan
Editor: Penelope Jackson
Editor for the press: Whitney Moran

Library and Archives Canada Cataloguing in Publication

Title: A great big night / words by Kate Inglis ; art by Josée Bisaillon.
Names: Inglis, Kate, 1973- author. | Bisaillon, Josée, illustrator.
Identifiers: Canadiana (print) 20200271091 | Canadiana (ebook) 20200271105 | ISBN
9781771089081 (hardcover) |
ISBN 9781771089098 (EPUB)
Classification: LCC PS8617.N52 G74 2020 | DDC jC813/.6—dc23

Nimbus Publishing acknowledges the financial support for its publishing activities from
the Government of Canada, the Canada Council for the Arts, and from the Province of
Nova Scotia. We are pleased to work in partnership with the Province of Nova Scotia to
develop and promote our creative industries for the benefit of all Nova Scotians.

For all the little frogs—
the musicians, artists, dreamers—
and their marvellous riff-raff.

-K.I.

Three travelling players
With tidy faces, winking eyes, and a gentle manner
Pedalled through the great green forest.

They rode painted bicycles

With a harpsichord on wagon wheels

A rat-a-tat tom-tom drum

A bump-biddie-bump-bitty bodhrán

And a shiny polished bucket

With a lovely rin-tin-tin upside-down sound.

And pockets full of whistles

A mandolin and two fiddles

A hundred-year-old golden guitar

A matchbox bass with a spider-silk bow

And a ukulele with stripes like a bumblebee.

Teeny-tiny cards in teeny tiny wheels went
Clickity-clackity-clickity-clack
As they pedalled through the great green forest.

The music train was a happy sight
Clickity-clackity three on bikes
Rolling in for a great big night.

"Oh!" said Rabbit. "I know that sound!"
Clickity-clackity-clickity-clack.

Old Crow cawed from the tamarack tree:
"Ca-caw! A show! They're here!
Porcupine a-prickle, Otter likes a tickle!
Ducks a clucky gaggle, Turtle's neck a-saggles!
Gather round!" And the crowd grew.

"Let's dance-a-doodle-doo!"

Fox said *shush* to Chickadee

"It's almost time!

Ta-whee-whee-whee!"

Frog One bowed deep with a tin-whistle grin

Then Frog Two with his mandolin blue

Frog Three lifted her tipper high and...

RAT-A-TAT-TAT! Began the great big night.

A jig for a giggle and a reel for a spin

A fling for to sing and a two-step stomp.

Claws and paws went

    Ka-thumpa-thump-thump!

Feathery wings went whap-whap-whap!

Squirrelly tails went swish-swish-swish!

Bear's big tummy ba-bompa-bomp-bomped.

So loud! So bouncy!
The grass was pounded flat.

Such fun for all—

except for one.

Grouse chortled over

In a very important kind of way

And the music stopped.

"Foolish racket!" he grouched.

"You do-nothings! Idlers! Loafers!

Lollygaggers, time-wasters, bah.

No good comes from a ruckus.

Not a lick of real work!

Make your ma proud

Lay off this...this...RIFF-RAFF!"

But my ma LOVES my riff-raff.

Then—a thunderclap! BOOM.
    A raindrop! PLOP.
Frog One shouted as the sky went dark:
"Go home now, skitter and skat!
Until next time you hear clickity-clack!"

The wind blew Bat to her cave
Fox tumble-splashed to his cozy hole
Finch held shivery-tight to a maple branch.
The northwest gale of angry black
Had its fist 'round pine and tamarack.
All the trees shook and cracked
    In the howling wind.

How the storm whipped and roared!
Little friends shivered, squished in hiding places
Feeling very small.

What a long and boggle-eyed night!

By dawn the storm was sleepy
From wind to whisper
Thunder to mist
Leaving little diamonds everywhere.
Aaaaaaah, sighed the trees
Under a soft pink sky.

Forest friends hugged with wobbly legs
And counted tiny eggs.
"Now here comes the sun!"

Such joy for all—except one.

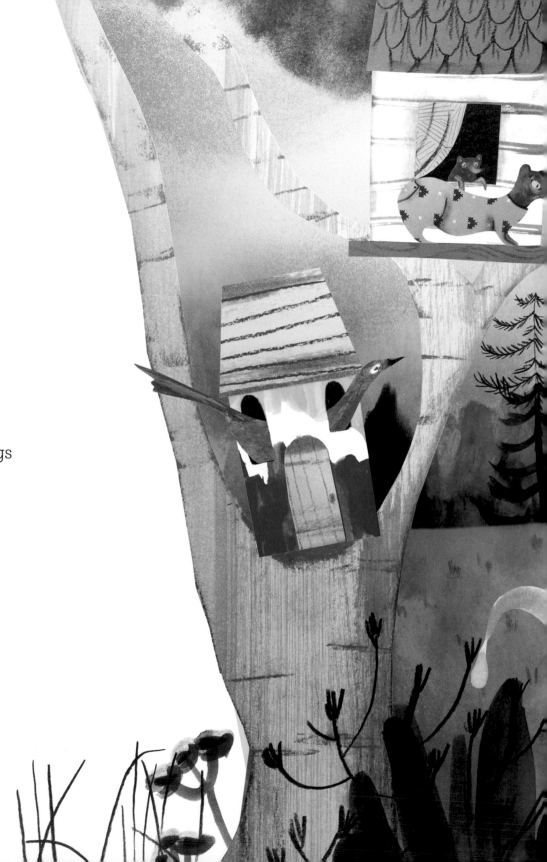

"Someone is crying!"

They found proud Grouse
    In a heap on the ground
His home and treasures all blown away.

"The shine on my shoes,
    Gold threads in my rug!
My silk bed bonnet, my King George mugs.
    Now all I am is a prince of mud!"

Oh dear, thought Frog Two. *What might I do for you?*
He was just that sort of frog.
He set down his teeny-tiny rucksack
And from it, pulled his fiddle.

"GO AWAY! DO NOT PLAY!" wailed Grouse.

Frog One joined with her golden guitar.

Three with her drum,
that thumpety-thump.

" HOW DARE YOU?
STOP IT, STOP IT RIGHT NOW!
CAN'T YOU SEE THIS IS
NO TIME FOR RIFF-RAFF ? "

Grouse didn't know, you see—
A rat-a-tat bump-ba-bump
Tippy-tapping tune
Does more than call for friends
To dance a doodle-doo.

Frog One began to sing a tune.

"Raven, with your inky black!
Hiding in the marsh, Muskrat!
Porcupine a-tip-top the willow tree
Duck and all your hatchlings wee
There is a friend in need
Bashed and battered by the storm!
Let's all work to make him warm."

Rabbit heard the Help! Help! song
And came running lickety-split.
Up the path pranced the new fawn
And Bear with a nice blueberry salad.
Very soon the air was filled with the knock-knock-bang
Of fixing and making brand new.
A scurry of chipmunks skipped along and said,
"HOWDY-DOO! What a mess!"

They skittered here and there
Sweeping and raking away
All the smashed bits
And starting a jolly little campfire.
The good clean smoke made everyone cheerful
And of course, the blueberry salad.

A little cottage appeared
As the happy beat of busy-time
songs filled the air.

"Riff-raff," sniffed Grouse
As he looked down
At his own tip-tapping toe—OH!

Four travelling players
With tidy faces, winking eyes,
And a gentle manner
Pedal through the great green forest.

Four, you say?
Not three? Indeed!
Grouse the fourth, on accordion
And wing-thrum drum
With a great big smile,
If a little sheepish.

The music train is a happy sight
Clickity-clackity four on bikes
Rolling in for a great big night.
Old crow caws from the tamarack tree:

"Ca-caw! A show! They're here!"